Andy, this one's for you!

First published in paperback in Great Britain by Collins Picture Books in 2002
First published in hardback and paperback in Great Britain, in this edition, by Collins Picture Books in 2003

3 5 7 9 10 8 6 4 2

ISBN: 0 00 714197 1

Collins Picture Books is an imprint of the Children's Division, part of HarperCollins Publishers Ltd.

Text and illustrations copyright © Mandy Stanley 2002

Visit our website at: www.harpercollinschildrensbooks.co.uk

Manufactured in China.

Lettice

The Flying Rabbit
Mandy Stanley

HarperCollins *Children's Books*

Lettice Rabbit and her family
lived high up on top of the hill.
Nibble, nibble, hop, hop, every day was the same.
   'Nothing ever happens here,' Lettice sighed,
rolling over on to her back.

Just then a small bird flew overhead.
Lettice watched as it swooped and looped high
over the meadow.

'I wish I could fly,' Lettice thought, 'but it could
only happen in my dreams.'

And Lettice thought how wonderful it would be to soar high into the sky, as light and free as a feather.

'Perhaps I can fly,' thought Lettice.
'I've never even tried.'

Lettice jumped
to her feet.

She flapped her arms,

she flapped her ears.

She even flapped her
whiskers and tail, but
nothing seemed to work.

Lettice flopped down on the grass, very fed up.

'I'll never be able to fly...' suddenly she stopped.
She could hear a strange, deep humming sound.

It was a beautiful pink aeroplane, turning and diving in the sky. 'Wow!' breathed Lettice and she jumped up and scampered after it.

She bounded across the meadow,

under the bramble hedge, over the stile

and through the stream, until, in the
distance, she saw the plane land.

Lettice hopped up to take a closer look.
Inside the cockpit was a tiny seat, just the
right size for a small rabbit. She had to try it.

Lettice wriggled her bottom into the seat. Suddenly the plane made a loud rumbling noise. It lurched forward and jolted up, up, up into the sky.

'Help!'
squealed Lettice.

As she tried to take a peek down below she could see fields and woods stretching far into the distance.

'I never knew the world was this big!' she gasped.

Just then a sudden gust of wind
pushed the little plane sideways.
'Uh, oh!' cried Lettice.

Judder,

Clank,

Whoosh,

went the plane.

And then...

CRASH!

The plane flew into a tree
in the middle of a wood,
a long way from home.

Lettice was thrown out.
She clung on to a branch,
dangling high
above the ground.

'I wish I was safe at home,'
she whispered, tearfully.

Lettice's arms ached and she couldn't
hold on any longer. Her paws slipped
and she began to fall
down

down

down...

...straight into the arms of a little girl.
'What are you doing in my plane?' laughed
the girl, putting her safely on the ground.

'I just wanted to be able
to fly,' sobbed Lettice,
'but it all went wrong and
now I'll never get home.'

'I can fly you back,' said the girl and she showed
Lettice the special control box
that made the plane fly.

'Oh, thank you,' squeaked Lettice. She took a
deep breath and climbed into the seat once again.
The engine started and the plane lifted smoothly
up into the air.

The plane took Lettice high above the wood.
She flew over the fields and river, and then her
very own meadow.

'I love flying!' Lettice squealed as she looped
the loop.

Down below, the Rabbit family looked up, amazed.

'It's Lettice,' they cried. 'Look, she's really flying!'

Once she had landed safely Lettice and her family
bounded back to the burrow.
   'We want to fly too!' cried her brothers and sisters,
clapping their paws as Lettice told them her story.

Lettice looked round, thinking she must be the happiest, and luckiest, rabbit in the world. 'Sometimes,' she thought, 'you really can make a dream come true.'

Lettice

Collect Mandy Stanley's adorable books about
Lettice - the little rabbit with big dreams!

0-00-716584-6

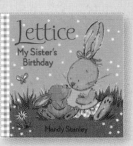

0-00-716583-8

0-00-716581-1

0-00-716582-X

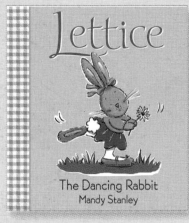

0-00-664777-4

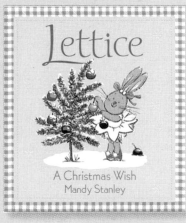

0-00-716585-4

Another dream comes
true for Lettice in
her next book, when she
becomes a bridesmaid!